GUS the BUS

by Olga Cossi
Illustrated by Howie Schneider

SCHOLASTIC INC. / New York

*To Bob McLaughlin and his third grade class at
Crown Elementary School in Coronado, California*
O.C.

For Zbignose
H.S.

Text copyright © 1989 by Olga Cossi
Illustrations copyright © 1989 by Howie Schneider
All rights reserved. Published by Scholastic Inc.
SCHOLASTIC HARDCOVER is a registered trademark
of Scholastic Inc.
Design by Meredith Dunham

Library of Congress Cataloging-in-Publication Data
Cossi, Olga.
Gus the Bus/by Olga Cossi: illustrated by Howie Schneider.   p. cm.
Summary: When a schoolbus has extra air put into his new tires, he
begins behaving most uncharacteristically.
ISBN 0-590-41616-2
[1. School buses—Fiction.]   I. Schneider, Howie, 1930-   ill.   II. Title.
PZ7.C819Gu 1989   [E]—dc19   88-14729
                                                             CIP
12 11 10 9 8 7 6 5 4 3 2 1   9/8 0 1 2 3 4/9   AC
Printed in the U.S.A.
First Scholastic printing, March 1989

At 7:15 A.M. on the dot, a bright yellow school bus turned the corner on Elm Street.

It was Gus the Bus, right on time.

He picked up the children, just as he was
supposed to, and went on his way. He had many
stops to make before he finished his run.

By 9:00 A.M. on the dot, Gus had made all his stops and taken his busload of children safely to Hilltop School, just as he was supposed to. He pulled into the parking lot so the Inspector could give him his daily checkup.

"Gus needs new tires," the Inspector told the driver. "Go to the Wheel Shop and see that he gets a new set of heavy-duty radials."

The driver drove Gus to the Wheel Shop. "Take off these old tires and put on a new set of heavy-duty radials," he told the workmen.

Then he went home to lunch.

The workmen put four new tires on Gus and filled them with air.

Then they went home to lunch.

Gus was happy with the new tires.
He couldn't wait to try them out. So
he started his engine and off he went.

The heavy-duty radials felt wonderful! They had so much air in them that Gus could zip around corners without squealing.

The rubber felt so thick, Gus could roll over bumps without rattling a single window.

The tread was so heavy-duty, Gus could go anywhere, even up the steepest hill, without slipping.

Gus felt like a new bus.

All of a sudden, a big, black dog rushed after Gus, barking and biting at his new set of tires.

Gus had never paid any attention before when dogs chased him. But he had never had a set of heavy-duty radials before, either.

Instead of going along as he was supposed to, Gus decided to race the dog. He revved up his motor and flashed his headlights. Then he stomped on his new tires. The dog was so surprised, he ran down the road as fast as his four legs could go. Gus was right on his tail.

Just when something terrible was about to happen, the big, black dog jumped up on the sidewalk and hid behind a house.

Gus went on his way again. But now there was a silly, wide grin across his radiator.

Gus headed for a country road he had always
wanted to try. He rode past a horse ranch, where
a few frisky colts were galloping across the
pasture. Just then, his headlights began to flash.

"I'll bet I can gallop, too, now that I have a new set of heavy-duty radials," Gus thought. He stomped on his

new tires and made a run for the fence. Over the top he went, landing with a bounce inside the pasture.

The colts took one look at the bus, threw back their heads, tossed their manes, and galloped away. Gus shifted into high gear and bounced around the pasture. The colts ran even faster, trying to keep ahead of the galloping bus.

Just when something terrible was about to happen, the colts headed for the barn, ran inside, and kicked the door closed behind them.

Gus bounced back over the fence and onto the road. Now he not only had a wide, silly grin across his radiator, but he had a bunch of wildflowers stuck in his rearview mirror, too.

All afternoon, Gus the Bus did things
he was not supposed to do.

He raced a red fire truck
to a four-alarm fire and

almost got there first!

He taxied down the runway at the airport and tried to take off like an airplane!

He turned a corner so fast he almost smashed into a mailbox.

By the time Gus the Bus returned to the Wheel
Shop, he had done so many things he was not
supposed to do, that even his heavy-duty radials
were tired.

But there was a very wide, silly grin across his
radiator when Gus settled down to wait for the
driver. Soon he was back at the Hilltop School
parking lot, ready for his afternoon run.

When the Inspector saw Gus, he came running over, shaking a fistful of papers. "Look at this!" he cried. "Look at all the complaints I got about you today! What have you been doing?

"Here is a complaint from the City Fire Chief, saying you raced Engine Number One to a four-alarm fire!

"And here is one from the airport for trying to fly without a license!

"And another from the United States Post Office for nearly smashing into a corner mailbox. . . .

"Why have you done all these things you were not supposed to do?" asked the Inspector.

Gus had been a model bus for years. He carried busloads of children to and from Hilltop School day after day without missing a single stop or being late. Why did he suddenly have a wide, silly grin across his radiator? And why was there a bunch of wildflowers sticking out of his rearview mirror?

The Inspector checked his daily records. He saw that Gus had been given a new set of heavy-duty radials that very morning. The tires did seem to be extra big and bouncy.

"A-ha!" he cried. "I see what's wrong. There is too much air in your tires!"

That afternoon, Gus took his busload of children home from school, just as he was supposed to.

The next morning, at 7:15 A.M. on the dot, the yellow school bus turned the corner at Elm Street. It was Gus the Bus, right on time for his first stop. He picked up the children and went on his way, just as he was supposed to.

By 9:00 A.M. on the dot, Gus had
made all his stops and was back in
the parking lot at Hilltop School,
ready for his daily checkup.

The first thing the Inspector did was check Gus's new set of heavy-duty radials. All four tires had exactly the right amount of air in them.

SCHOOL BUS

GUS 1

Everything else about Gus was just the way it was supposed to be.

Well, almost everything.

There were still some wildflowers sticking out of
his rearview mirror. And . . .

. . . across his radiator, Gus was still wearing a
wee bit of a silly grin.